**Leaving**

Large Lizzy had three Dragon-sized problems, and their names were Sparky, Flambo and Little Ignatius.

Her troubles began when the green speckled Dragon eggs she had laid a hundred years ago (and promptly forgotten) cracked open. Out popped the problems, howling loudly for licky lumps of coal and tasty titbits of firewood. Then began two hundred years of sleepless nights, which of course is no joke.

It wasn't so bad when the three little Dragons were still cute and cuddly and said 'ga ga' and 'blurk, tee hee' and tripped over their tails and giggled a lot. Large Lizzy taught them fire breathing and claw sharpening, and told them to cover their mouths when yawning and always wear a warm scarf in chilly weather.

She liked the way they snuggled up on cold winter nights and listened wide-eyed to the old Dragon tales and songs. The song they liked best of all was a lullaby, although when Dragons sing lullabies, NOBODY gets any sleep! It went like this:

*We'll fly to the Land of the Dragon*
*Forget all our troubles and toils*
*We'll while away hours picking snapdragon flowers*
*And snoring in squiggly coils.*

*Each Dragon that goes there is welcome*
*You'll find all the friendship you crave*
*In the wonderful Land of the Dragon*
*Where there's no need to hide in a cave.*

'Is it true, Ma?' the little Dragons would ask. 'Is there really such a place?'

'I doubt it,' Lizzy would reply. 'It's just an old song, that's all. All Dragons hide in caves these days. We're unpopular. Something to do with The Size. Bedtime now. Everyone cleaned their fangs?'

But those cosy evenings were long gone. Sparky and Flambo grew to the size of buses in no time at all. Two hundred years, actually, which is no time at all to a Dragon. Little Ignatius never seemed to get beyond the smallish-lorry stage, which was just as well because the cave was becoming horribly cramped.

It had started off as a perfect cave – well hidden half-way up a mountain, far away from People, and just the right size for one big green Dragon. It was, however, totally the wrong size for four.

Everyone got on each other's nerves and tripped over each other's coils. Major fires broke out every time someone coughed. There were sooty claw marks all over the walls. Sparky and Flambo were going through a horrible show-off stage, and lounged around demanding more dinner and picking on Little Iggy. Large Lizzy was getting very tired of it. She wanted to sleep, think, paint her talons and generally please herself. In fact, she wanted her home to herself again.

One night, her patience wore so thin that it finally snapped. The continual teasing of Little Iggy was the straw that finally broke the Dragon's back. Flambo started it.

'Look at Iggy. He's sucking his claw again.'

'Don't start,' warned Lizzy.

'No I'm not,' said Iggy, indignant. Though he was. Just a bit.

'He's a baby,' agreed Sparky. 'Only babies suck their claws.'

'I happen to have a small branch stuck in my teeth, that's all,' explained Iggy.

'Fibber,' said Sparky.

'Baby,' said Flambo.

'You heard me. SHUSH!' scolded Lizzy.

There was a short silence. Then:

'Iggy's crying,' said Flambo.

'No I'm not,' replied Iggy crossly.

'Cry Dragon,' taunted Sparky. 'Baby-waby cwy Dwagon.'

'I'm *not*,' insisted Iggy. 'I've got smoke in my eyes, that's all. Stop *breathing* all over me, Sparky.'

'Fibber,' said Sparky, breathing all over him.

'Baby,' added Flambo.

'ENOUGH!' growled Largy Lizzy, heaving about and thumping her rock pillow. 'Or else!'

There was another short silence. Then Sparky said, 'I'm hungry. I think I'll eat Iggy's twiglets.'

'Ma. Tell him,' complained Iggy, who had been saving them.

'I'm hungry too,' agreed Flambo. 'And thirsty. I want a drink of lava. With a straw. Ma, I want a drink of lava ...'

Two very angry looking jets of smoke spurted from Large Lizzy's nostrils.

'RIGHT! THAT DOES IT!' she boomed. 'Come on, the three of you. Clean your fangs, scrub your claws and put your scarves on. Get moving! We're going walking.'

Going walking?

In the middle of the night?

This was very odd.

Dragons, you see, rarely go out. They declare it's because they're unpopular, on account of The

6

Size, which is true, but really, it's pure laziness. Their short legs aren't built for walking, and they tend to waddle so that their stomachs scrape on the ground, which isn't much fun. When they do venture out, it's usually to get in huge supplies of food so they don't have to do it again for simply ages.

'Why?' rose the aggrieved cry. 'Why, Ma? Where?'

'Never you mind,' rumbled Lizzy grimly. 'Just get ready. And no more arguing, or I'll smack your tails. I mean it, mind!'

Outside, it was nearing daybreak. Fangs gleaming, claws scrubbed and scarves on, the three Dragons followed their mother up the mountain path. Sparky and Flambo were sulking and trailing their scarves in the mud on purpose. But Iggy was enjoying himself.

Iggy was an unusual Dragon. He wasn't really interested in the usual Dragon things: sleeping, dark caves, and long arguments when everyone got cross and breathed a lot of hot air. Those things bored him.

Only eating didn't bore him.

He liked that all right.

Iggy also liked walking. In fact, he would often sneak out for a little stroll when his mother and brothers were sleeping in a hot, cross tangle. He liked smelling the clean, fresh mountain air, and listening to the cheeps and rustles and small

scratchings of the Little Creatures going about their business. He envied the Little Creatures. They led such busy, interesting lives. He tried talking to them, but they just giggled and ran away. Sometimes they screamed or passed out, which was a bit upsetting as he was only trying to be friendly.

He sipped cold water from a mountain spring and hurriedly spat it out again. Water doesn't agree with Dragons. They prefer wood and coal, which keep their fires burning. He watched the bats and owls swoop past the moon, and wished he could fly like them. He even saw an Eagle once. He waved and yelled to it, and it smirked and did something unpleasant on his head. Eagles are like that.

This surprise family outing was a real treat for Iggy. He bit the top off a pine tree and hummed a little song.

'Dunno why you're so cheerful,' muttered Flambo. 'We only went for a walk the other day. My feet still hurt.'

'That was ten years ago,' Iggy pointed out.

'So? We got a lot in. We haven't eaten it all yet. Why go out again?'

'Perhaps it's a surprise picnic.'

'Where's the hamper then? Where's the hamper, stupid? I can't see a hamper. Can you see a hamper, Sparky?'

'No. Can you see my scarf?' said Sparky, looking worried. It suddenly didn't seem to be round his neck any more.

All three looked for Sparky's scarf. No amount of searching could find it, so Sparky snatched Iggy's, which was typical.

'Keep *moving* down there, you boys!' roared Large Lizzy. The three Dragons scampered to catch up. Startled bats and nesting birds rained from trees as the ground shook, and hundreds of rabbits and moles howled 'DRAGONQUAKE!' as their burrows caved in. A large boulder dislodged itself and went crashing off down the mountain-side, luckily only injuring itself. A sudden tidal wave in a nearby rock pool had a small, peacefully swimming water rat *really* worried for a moment.

'Slow down, Ma,' begged Sparky. 'We're exhausted.'

'You can rest now. We've reached the top.'

The three Dragons panted up the last little bit and joined Lizzy, who was crouched at the edge, peering out over a terrifying drop.

As dawn approached, the rays of the rising sun tipped the treetops of a great forest far below. They shone on the golden towers of a mighty palace far off in the distance. They glittered on the surface of a wide river winding its slow, sleepy way towards the far horizon. They warmed the ancient stones of a tumbledown castle on the outskirts of the tiny village nestling in the valley beneath.

'See that?' said Large Lizzy. 'Down there's the World.'

Sparky and Flambo looked unimpressed. They said it was very nice, and when was breakfast? Iggy said nothing. He just looked.

'Boys,' said Large Lizzy. 'Boys, guess what happens now? You're going to jump off.'

'Pardon?' asked Sparky and Flambo and Iggy together.

'Jump off,' repeated Lizzy. 'Isn't that fun?'

There was a long silence.

'Oh, really, you three!' sighed Lizzy, exasperated. 'Use your brains. What do you think your wings are for?'

The three Dragons looked at each other uncertainly. A Dragon's wings are the last thing to grow, and until recently they weren't much more than funny little lumps on the back. They hadn't been used for anything really, except swatting flies and scratching the odd itch in that awkward place where neither claws nor tail could reach.

'They're for Flying,' explained Large Lizzy. 'Just like the birds.'

'You said Dragons don't Fly any more,' protested Sparky.

'No I didn't,' said Lizzy.

'I'm sure you did, Ma. You said Dragons don't Eat Princesses or Fight Noble Knights or Guard Treasure any more. Or Fly.'

'I said they didn't, cheeky,' snapped Large Lizzy. 'Much. I didn't say they couldn't.'

'You mean we *can* Eat Princesses?' said Sparky, rather struck with the idea.

'Certainly not! It's bad manners. Besides, the crown gets stuck in your throat.'

'Let's get back to this Flying business,' broke in Iggy, nearly bursting with excitement. 'What do we have to do, Ma?'

'Nothing to it. You just flop off, open wide and flap. Like this.'

And before the Dragons could say 'Holy Smoke,' Lizzy launched herself over the edge, opened her strong wings, and was away, flying off into the rising sun.

'Wow!' breathed Sparky, Flambo and Iggy, watching their gleaming, golden mother ride the morning breeze.

'Wow! Look at Ma!'

Lizzy finally swooped back in a great gust of wind, circled around their heads, looped the loop and landed beside them.

'That's how you Fly,' she said casually. 'Now. Have you all got your scarves?'

'Iggy hasn't,' chorused Sparky and Flambo meanly.

'It's lucky I've brought a spare then,' said Large Lizzy. 'I don't want you catching colds five minutes after you leave home.'

What was this?

Leave home?

Now? This minute?

'Listen, boys,' said Lizzy. 'You can't stay home any more. You're too big. Today's the day you must fly away.'

'But . . .'

'No arguments. You have to learn to stand on your own four claws. Of course, I shall be pleased to get a visit from you – say, in two hundred years time, when I've caught up on my sleep. Don't forget the bunch of flowers. Now, if you take my advice, you'll find a nice dark cave, get in a good supply of coal and firewood, get plenty of sleep and stay away from People, particularly Knights and Princesses. Dragons just aren't popular. It's . . .'

'Something to do with The Size,' mumbled Sparky, Flambo and Iggy tearfully.

'Quite. Now, who's going first?'

'Iggy,' said Sparky and Flambo together, hastily shuffling back from the edge. Flying looked wonderful when Large Lizzy did it. It also looked highly dangerous.

Iggy didn't mind. In fact, he couldn't wait to have a go. He would be sad to leave Large Lizzy, of course – but at the same time, how exciting it all was. How glorious to touch the moon with a wing tip, chase among the stars, slide down a rainbow and bounce on the clouds. Maybe get his own back on that Eagle. What fun to be on his own for a while, with no one to boss him around. He imagined eating his way through tons of coal and whole forests of firewood without Sparky and Flambo pinching all the best bits. And when he'd done all that – then what?

Then, maybe, he'd search for the Land of the Dragon. He liked the sound of a land where Dragons were welcome, and didn't have to hide all the time.

'All right,' he said.

'Here goes,' he said.

'Er . . . I'll just try out my wings, then,' he said.

'Get on with it, cissy,' jeered Sparky and Flambo.

Iggy moved to the edge and looked down. Suddenly, he wasn't so sure. The ground seemed very far below. Suppose his wings didn't work?

Suppose when wings were given out to Dragons his pair was the faulty pair, the pair that didn't . . .

'Go on, son,' encouraged Large Lizzy. 'Trust me. Open them out and give them a trial flap.'

Taking a deep breath, Iggy opened his wings.

He didn't mean to knock Sparky and Flambo off the edge. It merely happened that way because the opened-out wings were much bigger and stronger than he expected.

The big, strong, opened-out wings caught Sparky and Flambo squarely on the back of their necks and swept them forward, out and down before they could even cry out.

'O Ma!' gasped Iggy. 'What have I done?'

'Nothing to worry about,' said Large Lizzy. 'Watch. You'll see.'

Far below, two little black dots were getting smaller and smaller.

Then the two little dots sprouted wings, and began to grow bigger.

'Coming up!' bellowed Flambo, shooting up past them and doing a fancy twirl just above their heads, like the show-off he was. 'Look at me, Ma!'

'Whhheeeeee! This is fun,' shrieked Sparky. 'Mind your noses!'

'I'm off cave hunting now!' bawled Flambo. 'Goodbye, Ma! Goodbye Iggy! See you in two hundred years!'

'Wait for me! I'm coming with you!' howled Sparky. And with that, they zoomed away.

Two mud-stained scarves fluttered to the ground.

'Typical,' said Lizzy, and wiped her eyes with them.

'Ma,' said Iggy, watching his brothers vanish

into the sun. 'Sing me that song again. The one about Dragonland.'

'Get along with you,' said Large Lizzy, blowing her nose.

'Please.'

'Oh – bother the child. All right. How did it go again?'

She cleared her throat and began to sing. The rusty roar echoed across the mountain.

*Let's fly to the Land of the Dragon*
*Forget all our troubles and toils,*
*We'll while away hours picking snapdragon flowers*
*And snoring in squiggly coils.*

*We'll gossip with friends and with neighbours*
*We'll listen and learn to be wise,*
*To be proud of our wings and all Dragonish things*
*Like our Scales and our Tails and our Size.*

'Thanks, Ma.' said Iggy. 'I'll miss you. I'll send you a postcard when I get there.'

'You mean, *if* you get there.' said Lizzy. 'But good luck, son. Here. Take this scarf. Wrap it round on chilly nights, mind.'

And Iggy took the scarf, closed his eyes, took a deep breath . . .

AND JUMPED!

## 2

## Treasure

'What is it, Stu?' said a small voice somewhere near his ear.

'Well, I'll go out on a limb an' say it's a Dragon, Sid,' said another voice. 'On account of The Size.'

'Oh my pickled pine cones! You reckon? One of them from up the mountain, I s'pose. I 'eard there was a few up there.'

'Pity this one didn't stay there. 'Stead of spoilin' our branch.'

'Don't look well, do it? Try the kiss of life, Stu.'

'Nuts. You seen them fangs?'

Iggy felt tiny little feet jumping about on his stomach. They were light, but scratchy. They tickled.

'What we gonna do wiv it then?' said Sid irritably. 'It can't stay 'ere, can it? Not on our branch.'

'True,' said Stu. 'I mean, we was 'ere first,' he added.

'You said it, Stu. Never invited it, did we?'

'No way, Sid. Just come crashin' out of the sky, didn't it? Didn't even say 'scuse me, mind if I drop in. A real cheek.'

'Know what I fink, Stu? I fink we should push it off.'

'I'd rather you didn't, if you don't mind,' said Iggy, opening his eyes.

There were two shrill squeaks of alarm, and the scratchy little feet could no longer be felt. Iggy looked up, and saw leaves. He looked around, and saw more leaves. He looked down – and there was the ground, some way below, scattered with broken branches. He was lying on his back on a big branch half way up a tall oak tree, and his head hurt. He tried shifting a little, and found that his other end hurt as well. From a safe distance along the branch, two small grey Squirrels stared at him with round, startled eyes.

'Sorry about this,' said Iggy politely. 'I understand this is your branch.'

The Squirrels just stared some more.

'I suppose I must have crash landed,' he added. 'I'm not that good at Flying yet. Hold tight, I'm going to try sitting up.'

It was a struggle, untangling himself from the surrounding foliage. His scarf was caught on a twig, nearly strangling him as he finally fought his way into a sitting position with his back against the stout trunk.

'That's better. I must have looked a bit silly lying on my back like that,' he said with a little laugh.

'You still look silly,' remarked a Squirrel. 'With that bird's nest on your head.'

Feeling foolish, Iggy removed several clawfuls of straw from his head. It was all coming back to him now. He remembered jumping off the mountain, and the wonderful feeling of stretching wide his wings and Flying for the first time.

He remembered the wind whistling past as he dived and swooped and did clever little twirls and twiddles.

He remembered turning somersaults.

He remembered trying it upside down and backwards.

He remembered . . .

DOING IT WITH HIS EYES CLOSED!

'I tried Flying with my eyes closed,' he explained sheepishly. 'I must have been lower than I thought. I'm sorry about your tree.'

'So you should be,' snapped Stu.

'Look at the damage you've done,' added Sid. 'See them nuts down there all over the ground?

Those was our nuts, wasn't they Stu?'

'Off our branch, Sid,' agreed Stu.

'Well, you can still eat them, can't you? I'll help you pick them up . . .'

'Not ripe. Not by a long shot. Ruined, them nuts.'

'Oh dear. Well, perhaps I can pay for them or something . . .'

'With what?' said Stu.

'What with?' said Sid.

'With – oh dear, I'm afraid I haven't got anything on me right now. Except my scarf, but I'm rather fond of that.'

'Poo! What good's an old scarf to a Squirrel?' snorted Sid rudely. 'Look, mate, you're in the wrong. Breaking and entering it's called. Ain't that right, Stu?'

'Look, if there's anything I can do . . .' offered Iggy, feeling guilty.

'Well, what can you do?' asked Stu.

'It can't fly, that's for sure,' said Sid rudely. Iggy ignored that.

'I can breathe fire,' he offered. 'If you want any fires started . . .'

'What good's that to us?'

'Well – roasted chestnuts are rather nice . . .' said Iggy weakly.

'No thanks. What else? Apart from make a nuisance of yerself?'

Iggy thought. What could Dragons do? Eat? Sleep?

'Guard Treasure,' he said firmly. 'Yes, we're very good at Guarding Treasure.'

Stu and Sid looked at each other thoughtfully. They whispered a bit, bushy grey tails twitching. Finally, they reached a decision. Stu spoke.

'Fair enough, mate. We got a little guarding job you can do for us, matter of fact.'

'But can it be trusted?' added Sid, sounding doubtful.

'Of course,' said Iggy, shocked. A Dragon who couldn't be trusted! Whatever next?

'Right. Well, crane yer neck around a bit, towards the trunk. See that 'ole by yer left ear?'

Iggy craned his neck and saw the hole.

'Yes,' he said. 'Definitely.' He wanted to sound businesslike, as this was his first proper job.

'Well, that there 'ole's full of last year's nut hoard, see? Them nuts is the best for miles about, an' there's plenty'd like to get their paws on 'em. Know what I mean?'

'Absolutely,' nodded Iggy.

'An' me an' Sid can't leave the branch. Else you know what'd 'appen, don't yer?'

'They'd get stolen.' explained Sid. 'By some nut,' he added.

'Tch tch tch,' tutted Iggy with a little laugh to show he understood the joke.

'So how's about keepin' yer eye on it for a bit? Give us a chance to nip out and make a few trunk calls? Have a natter, you know, bit of a chinwag. Catch up on the gossip.'

'I'd be delighted,' said Iggy. 'Rely on me.'

'Right then. Do a proper job, and we'll forget about the damage. Coming, Sid? We'll get a few nuts in while we're about it. Add to the hoard.'

'Suits me,' said Sid, with a wink at Iggy. 'I love doing nutting.'

And with a flash of their tails, they were gone.

Iggy shuffled around on the branch, so that he could keep a proper eye on the hole. Despite his bumps and bruises, he felt wonderful. Why, he'd only just left home, and already he'd got – no, he'd *fallen* into a job. He gave a little chuckle. He must remember to tell that joke to Large Lizzy in two hundred years time. Meanwhile, how good it felt to be doing something useful, something Dragons were good at. Guarding. What could be nicer?

An hour later, when he got cramp in his left foot, he began to think of one or two things which, frankly, might be nicer than Guarding.

Two hours later, when there was still no sign of the Squirrels or better still a thief, he'd thought of a whole list of things which he'd sooner do than Guard. The list went:

*1 Eat*
*2 Not sit in a tree*
*3 Find a cave and sleep*
*4 Have another go at flying (keeping eyes open)*
*5 Wash scarf*

Three hours later, when the moon rose and the dew fell, and the list was as long as his tail, he was stiff, cold, bored and POSITIVELY STARVING. Dragons need *loads* to eat, and poor Iggy hadn't had anything since the day before. What made it worse, all around him was good, solid nourishment, crunchy branches and tender little twiglets. But it didn't seem polite to eat the tree he was sitting in. His crash landing had already spoilt it rather a lot, and the branch he was sitting on belonged to his employers. It doesn't do to eat your employers' home.

He picked one tiny little twig and chewed it guiltily. He made it last for as long as he possibly could, which was about half a second. It was lovely, but not very filling. He was just reaching for a second, when a sound below made him snap to attention.

It was a rumbling, jingling, clanking, squeaking sound with the occasional cough mixed in. It was the kind of sound that might be made by a strange little man in a tall hat, pushing a ricketty handcart, hung about with pots and pans, across a forest glade. Which is, of course, exactly what it was. Iggy held his breath as the spiderlike figure came to a halt directly beneath his tree. He'd never seen a People close up before. He'd seen them from a distance, of course. Tiny, feeble, little creatures who tended to point and faint.

Iggy examined the People closely. He was wearing raggedy trousers, a patched cloak, and battered boots with the soles flapping loose. A dirty red hanky was tied around his scrawny neck, and crafty little eyes peered from beneath the tall black hat.

'Fire first,' muttered the People. 'Get meself all warmy toasty, yep!'

Iggy watched as the People scuttled about piling up broken branches.

He watched the People take a kettle from the cart, fill it with water from a nearby brook and place it on the pile.

He watched the People search for something to light the fire with.

He watched the People fail to find it.

He watched the People get very cross indeed.

Iggy began to feel rather sorry for the shivering, mumbling, unhappy little People. He obviously needed help.

'Excuse me,' he called down in a gentle voice, so as not to startle the little fellow.

'Do you need a light?'

The People looked up, screamed, leaped into the air and landed flat on his back, where he lay gibbering in a state of shock. It's not surprising. Imagine being in a deep dark forest at night, thinking you are all alone, then all of a sudden a Dragon the size of a lorry leans down from an oak tree and offers you a light.

'I'm awfully sorry,' called down Iggy. 'I didn't mean to scare you.'

The People merely waved his legs around like an overturned crab, and mumbled something.

'Pardon? I didn't quite catch that,' said Iggy.

'Go away. I said GO AWAY,' croaked the People.

'I can't,' explained Iggy. 'I'm busy. Look, please get up. I really won't hurt you.'

Slowly, the People sat up. Nothing terrible happened, so he stood. His legs sagged a bit, but apart from that he seemed all right.

'Is it a Dragon you are?' he enquired, peering up at Iggy. 'Is it a Dragon a-hiding up there in the shadows and a-booming at me?'

'Yes. I was only trying to help. I thought you wanted to light your fire.'

'Have you some matches then?'

'We Dragons don't need matches,' said Iggy proudly. 'We breathe fire.'

'Oh you do, do you? Well, fire away then. But mind me.'

The fires were burning very low indeed in Iggy's stomach, because he hadn't eaten for such a long time. However, with a great effort, he managed to produce one little spark which he blew in the direction of the woodpile. It was small and feeble, but it did the trick. The People looked a lot happier as the branches caught alight and the kettle began to sing.

'Well, well. Yep! Will you look at that. 'Course,

I heard tell you lot breathed fire. I niver knowed you slept in trees, though. Nope.'

'We don't. I'm not sleeping.'

'What you a-doing of then? Waiting for apples to grow?'

'No. I'm Guarding.'

'Oh? Guarding, is it? Guarding what?' The People's eyes had an even craftier look.

'Treasure,' said Iggy.

'Tell you what,' said the People, suddenly very friendly. 'Why don't you come on down? Yep. Join me by the fire. I've niver had a close look at a Dragon see. You can Guard just as well from down here, can't you? I'll be a-cooking a sausage or two in a bitsy. Fancy one?'

Iggy thought. It was true. He could Guard just as easily at the foot of the tree. He'd never eaten a sausage, but he liked the sound of it. Besides, there was all that firewood lying around. The Squirrels would probably be very pleased if he made an effort to tidy it up.

'All right,' he said. 'Thanks. Stand back, I'm going to jump.'

The People moved hastily out of the way as Iggy launched himself off the branch and sailed down. He landed with a great crashing belly flop which caused the ground to shudder and the kettle to tumble off the fire.

'You're a fair old size,' said the People, setting

the kettle upright again.

'I'm quite small, actually,' said Iggy modestly. 'For a Dragon.'

'Well, you're big enough for me. Have you got a name?'

'Ignatius. Iggy for short.'

'Big Iggy, eh? Well, Iggy, a big chap like you could probably eat two sausages, I imagine. Or even three, yep?'

'Yes please.' Iggy found himself liking the People more and more. Big Iggy. It was rather good. Grand sounding.

'Well, sit yourself down then, while I cook.'

'Er – do you mind if I help myself to a snack while we're waiting? I'm a bit peckish.'

'What sort o' snack?' said the People, edging backwards and looking uncomfortable.

'Well, there are all these broken branches going spare, unless of course, you . . .?'

'Eh? Oh, I see. Oh no, no, ha, ha, people don't eat firewood, friend. Help yourself. Yep.'

The People watched curiously for a moment while Iggy crunched his way greedily through a branch or two, then busied himself at his cart.

'About this Treasure you're a-guarding,' he said pleasantly, returning to the fire with a handful of sausages and a frying pan. 'What sort o' Treasure did you say it was again? Up there? In the tree?'

'I didn't,' said Iggy.

'Oh no, 'course you didn't, nope, ha, ha. I was just interested. You know, I was just sort of casually a-wondering. A diamond necklace, perhaps? I know magpies steal 'em from time to time. Or might it be a bag o' gold, mmm? Hidden there by robbers until such time as they need it? Or is it a secret, eh? Well, I can keep secrets. You'll whisper it later, I dare say. Now, how many sausages, my friend? Ten?'

'If you can spare them.'

'Oh, certainly, certainly. We'll have a mug o' tea later too. We're friends, eh? All chummy-chummy. I mean, you done me a good turn. Old Shamus don't forget his friends.'

'Is that your name?'

'Yep. Shamus O'Shifty. Traveller, pedlar, and mender o' pots and pans. To Royalty.'

'You're the first People I've ever talked to, Mr O'Shifty,' said Iggy.

'The first . . .? Oh, I see. You mean Person. One People is a Person. Call me Shamus.'

'I see,' nodded Iggy, pleased to be learning things. 'Shamus.'

'You know, Big Iggy, there's things Old Shamus could teach you about the world. Oh yep. There ain't much Old Shamus don't know. Nope. Here. Try one.'

Iggy tried his first-ever sausage.

He liked it.

He liked it A LOT.

'Good, eh?' said Shamus O'Shifty with a wink. 'Yep, I'd be pleased to tell you anything you care to know. 'Course, there's a thing or two I could learn from you. It's not often I meet a Dragon. Help yourself, friend, help yourself.'

Iggy helped himself.

'About this Guarding business, for example,' continued Shamus O'Shifty. 'You were a-telling me about the Treasure up there. In the tree.'

'I was?' said Iggy, stuffing sausages greedily.

'Yep. Don't you remember? I was a-trying to guess what it was, just for fun, you know, and you were a-going to tell me.'

'Nuts,' said Iggy.

'Eh? Look there's no need to be rude, chummy.'

'It's nuts, Shamus. The Treasure. I'm Guarding a nut hoard for two Squirrels.'

Iggy was very surprised when the sausage he was just about to pop into his mouth was snatched away.

'I'll take that,' snapped Shamus O'Shifty. 'Don't want to be greedy, do we? An' it's Mr O'Shifty to you!'

Iggy waited as Shamus O'Shifty chewed the last sausage in sullen silence. Somehow, he didn't seem quite so friendly.

'Nuts! Huh!' he muttered at last, licking his dirty fingers. 'You don't know what Treasure is, lizard. I could tell you a thing or two about Treasure. Oh yep. Old Shamus knows real Treasure when he sees it. I suppose you think you're clever. A-telling me there's Treasure up there.'

'No I don't,' said Iggy, not at all sure what he'd done to annoy his new friend.

'Nuts. Wasting my time. Eating my sausages. Huh. You've got a lot to learn, chummy. About *real* Treasure. You won't get far in this world a-guarding a load o' nuts for a couple o' mangy Squirrels.'

'Do you know about Real Treasure then, Mr O'Shifty?'

'Know about it? I got some. I could show you Treasure that'd make your eyes drop out. But I'm not going to. So there.'

And with that, Shamus O'Shifty snatched the frying pan from the fire and stomped off towards the brook, muttering furiously to himself. Iggy sighed. It didn't look as though he was going to be offered a mug of tea after all. He didn't know what tea was, but if it tasted anything like sausages, he would have loved some. He must have done or said something to upset Mr O'Shifty, but he had no idea what it was. If only he could make it up to him. But how?

He got to his feet and began to stroll around the

glade. Walking always made him think better. Besides, it would help the food go down. After a few lumbering exercises, he came to a halt by Shamus O'Shifty's handcart. He examined it curiously.

Dozens of pots, pans, kettles and buckets hung on hooks at the sides, and the cart was filled with various bulky sacks and battered boxes. Idly, he peeped into a sack. It was stuffed with old rags – probably the tinker's Sunday best clothes. He lifted the lid of one of the boxes. It contained a carved brass doorknob, two silver egg cups and dozens of paper-wrapped bars of soap, all emblazoned with the message:

PALACE PROPERTY. DO NOT REMOVE.

Odd.

The next sack also contained rags. But there was something else stuffed at the bottom. Something hard and round, that glittered . . .

'Oi!' came the shout. 'Get away from that cart, you! That cart's none o' your business!'

Just then, the kettle that had been singing away merrily on the fire boiled over. There was a great deal of hissing, and the fire went out. Iggy perked up. Now there was something he could do to make Mr O'Shifty like him again. He could relight the fire. He gave the sacks a little tidy, and hurried back to the damp pile.

He took a deep breath, and blew really hard.

That was where he made his mistake.

The fires in his belly were raging by now, because of all the branches he had consumed during his little snack. A fierce jet of flame blazed from his mouth, taking him by surprise.

Shamus O'Shifty's wet little woodpile caught alight again straight away. So did the oak tree containing the nut hoard which Iggy was supposed to be Guarding.

'Oh no!' he whispered, as the fire snaked up the trunk. 'Oh no!'

Horrified, he watched the flames streak along the branches. There was a crackling sound, and the unmistakable smell of roasting nuts. What was he to do? He tried to think. Fire. What put out fires? Water! Of course! He needed water!

Falling over his feet, he galloped back to the cart, and seized a bucket. He would fill the bucket with water, that's it, and throw it over the fire.

Then he would wet his scarf and put it over his nose so that he could climb up the tree and rescue the Squirrels' nut hoard.

It was a desperate plan. It was also a very bad one, for these reasons:

1 A blazing oak tree needs a lot more than one bucket of water to put it out.

2 Climbing up such a tree, even if you're a Dragon with a wet scarf over your nose, is *not* a good idea.

3 The bucket had a hole in it.

However, it was all Iggy could think of, so he went rushing off to the brook where Shamus O'Shifty stooped scrubbing out his greasy frying pan.

'What's all the rush about?' growled Shamus O'Shifty. 'Here, who are you a-pushing?'

'Sorry!' gasped Iggy. 'Need water. Bit of an accident.'

'Eh? Accident? What accid . . . oh my galloping granny! Fire! FIRE!'

'I know, I know! Oh bother, this bucket's got a hole! Excuse me, if I can just wet my scarf ...'

'YOUR SCARF? Can't you see there's a fire, you great dafty, dozey dummy of a Dragon? And you're washing your *scarf*?'

'Not wash! Wet! You see, I can put it over my nose and climb up and try to save the nuts ...'

'Nuts? Are you mad? What about my CART, dolt head? MY CART!'

And he dropped the frying pan and went running back as fast as he could to where the oak tree blazed like a beacon in the night.

Iggy swished his scarf about in the cold brook, placed it over his nose, and charged after him. As he reached the glade, there was a great clattering and clanking, and Shamus O'Shifty came staggering out of the thick smoke, pulling his handcart behind him. His hat was gone, his eyes were red and streaming, his face was covered with dirt and sweat, and altogether he didn't look too pleased.

'I'm awfully sorry ...' began Iggy.

'Sorry? SORRY?' screamed Shamus O'Shifty. 'You will be, chummy. I'll see to that. And you've been a-rummaging about on my cart, ain't you? I can tell. There's things been disturbed. You been a-poking around, looking at things what don't concern you. I'll have the law on you, I will. You're a fire hazard. A flaming nuisance! That's the last time I give sausages to a fire hazard. Out of my way!' And he ran his cart over Iggy's tail and made off into the night, screeching insults that caused Iggy to blush with shame.

There was no point in trying to save the nuts now, of course. The tree was blazing beautifully. It seemed as though the whole forest would be set alight. What a disaster.

Iggy took the wet scarf from his nose and wept into it. He had failed. He had failed at Flying, Guarding and Fire Lighting. Doubtless he'd fail at everything he turned his claw to. He was that sort of Dragon. Perhaps he'd better find a cave to crawl into after all. Oh dear. Ohdearohdearohdear.

While Iggy sat and wept in the burning glade, a Good Thing happened. A rainstorm put the fire out.

He was so depressed, he didn't even notice.

## 3

## A Princess

The small girl found him in exactly the same position the following morning. His huge green head rested on his knees and one claw still limply clutched the scarf. His eyes were closed, and, despite his size, he looked young and forlorn and sort of sweet. The small girl hesitated, then reached up and tapped him on the nose.

'Hey,' she said. 'Wakey, wakey!'

Iggy started, sneezed, and opened his eyes. He found himself staring down at a small Person with long, tangled brown hair and a freckled face. The dress she was wearing looked as though it had been a rather nice dress once. Blue, perhaps, with frills. Now it was a rather dirty grey colour with blobby mud splashes. The hem was torn, and the frills drooped in a way frills shouldn't. She was holding a grubby velvet drawstring bag in one hand. The oddest thing about her, though, was that she was wearing a huge black false moustache.

'Hello,' said the small girl. 'Sorry to wake you. Did you make this mess?'

Iggy stared through bleary eyes at the glade. Charred bushes and blackened trees still smouldered in a sea of sooty mud. The Squirrels' oak tree was no more than a smoking stump. It was still raining – a thin, spiteful, drippy drizzle. He felt like he had a cold coming on, and now he had to be polite to a strange small Person wearing a false moustache. Life was hard.

'Yes. I'm afraid . . . A . . . TCHOO!' A sad little spray of sparks shot from his mouth and fizzled out in a puddle.

'You've got a cold,' remarked the small girl. 'That's what comes of sleeping in puddles. What happened?'

'Bit of an a . . . A . . . Accident. CHOO! Mr O'Shifty didn't have a light, you see, and I . . .'

'Wait! Did you say O'Shifty?'

'ATCHOO! Yes.'

'Aha,' said the small girl grimly. 'Then I'm on the right trail.'

'Why? Is he a friend of yours?'

'Friend? Certainly not! He's a criminal, and I'm trailing him.'

'Really?' said Iggy. 'Well, I don't think he's my friend either. Not any more.'

'Good,' said the small girl. 'You look much too sensible to be friends with someone like that. What's your name? I might need you as a witness. I should warn you, anything you say may be taken down and used as evidence.'

'Lit . . . *Big* Iggy,' said Iggy. 'I'm a Dragon.'

'I thought so,' said the small girl. 'Something to

do with The Size. Well, Big Iggy, nice to meet you. Now I must be off. Which way did he go?'

'That way,' said Iggy, pointing. 'But wait! I don't even know your name.'

'Matilda,' called the small girl over her shoulder. 'I'm a detective. Oh, and a Princess.' And she vanished into the trees.

A Princess?

A PRINCESS?

'Come back!' shouted Iggy. 'Matilda! Wait for me!' And he charged after her, past the toasted trees and through the barbequed bushes.

'Hurry up if you're coming,' said Matilda, not pausing as he came wheezing and sneezing up behind her. 'I can't afford to dawdle now he's got a head start. Watch out for the cartwheel tracks. And try to be a bit quieter.'

Iggy obediently walked on tipclaw (difficult for a Dragon) and pinched his nose to stifle the sneezes. Matilda gave him one of those important, Warning Looks. The sort of Look given when the talk is about Walking Into Danger. A BEWARE sort of Look.

'Beware,' said Matilda, doing the Look. 'Come with me, and you Walk Into Danger.'

Iggy was terribly impressed, and wanted to know why.

'Because,' said Matilda. 'Because it's a dangerous sort of situation I'm in, that's why. I Walk

On A Razor's Edge. Trouble Is My Middle Name.
Play With Fire and You'll Get Burned. See?'

Iggy didn't see, but he liked the way Matilda
talked. It wasn't at all how he imagined a Princess
would talk. He was even more thrilled when she
took a large magnifying glass from her dirty velvet
bag and examined the forest floor, just like a real
detective.

'You're not a bit like I thought a Princess was,'
he said shyly. 'I like the moustache. It's – unusual.'

'Good,' said Matilda, tossing her hair with
satisfaction. 'Most princesses are very boring.
Hold this glass, I want to dust for footprints.' And
she took out a large pot and sprinkled white powder
around while Iggy sneezed and begged to know
why princesses were boring.

'Because they just sit around in soppy dresses
all day and never go on adventures. Just as I
thought. He's heading North. Come on.'

'Is that what you're on?' asked Iggy eagerly, trotting after her. 'An adventure? A – TCHOO!'

'SSSSSH!' hissed Matilda with a warning scowl. 'The trees have ears. Even the bushes might be bugged.'

Bugged?

What sort of bugs?

Itchy ones or stingy ones?

Not ... *Squashy ones?*

Iggy wanted to know more about the bugs, but Matilda waved him silent.

'Shhhh! Voices up ahead.' They both froze. Matilda dropped to all fours, inched forward and peeped around the next tree.

'It's all right,' she called. 'Just a couple of grey Squirrels.'

'Oh no!' said Iggy. 'SSSSSSSHHHHHHH!' And they both froze again.

A few minutes later, when Iggy was nearly dead from trying to hold back a sneeze, Matilda risked another look.

'All clear, they've gone. Why are you hiding from a couple of grey Squirrels, a great thing like you?'

'I'll explain later,' said Iggy. 'It's all part of my adventure. A – A -ahhhhh ... ch ... ahhhh ... Funny, I don't want to sneeze now. The shock cured my cold.'

'What adventure? You're on one too?'

'Of course,' said Iggy, and explained all about leaving home and the crash landing and the Squirrels and Shamus O'Shifty and the accident and the Land of the Dragon. While he spoke, the rain stopped and the sun came out.

'It sounds lovely,' said Matilda, stopping in a leafy glade. 'Rest time now. At ease.' She sat on one end of a fallen branch, and Iggy eagerly bit into the other. While he ate, Matilda took a bright red, short-haired wig from her velvet bag, followed by a brush. She brushed the wig energetically. 'I like the sound of the last bit. The Land of the Dragon. Can only Dragons go there?'

'I think so,' said Iggy apologetically. 'Perhaps there's a Land of Princesses,' he added.

'Uggh! No thanks. I'll stick with bringing Shamus O'Shifty to justice, and getting back my crown.'

'Crown?' said Iggy. 'He's stolen your crown?'

'Mmm. I don't care that much, actually, except that Daddy'll be furious. It's the third one he's bought me this year.'

'He must be very rich,' gasped Iggy through a mouthful of log.

'Kings are,' said Matilda with a shrug. 'But he spends his money on silly things. I got a tiny golden coach for my birthday. With red cushions, and a white pony to pull it.'

'That sounds a lovely present,' breathed Iggy.

'Huh. Not what I wanted.'

'What did you want?'

'A new detective kit with a full set of disguises,' explained Matilda. 'I can't go on wearing this moustache for ever. Everyone's getting to recognise me. The wig's too small as well. Have you nearly finished, Iggy? O'Shifty's getting further away all the time.'

'How did he steal your crown?' asked Iggy, playing for time.

'Well,' said Matilda. 'I was leaning through the window yesterday morning, wondering whether to practise my stalking on one of the palace guards or write myself a letter in invisible ink. Just then, I saw Shamus O'Shifty down below. He comes to mend the kitchen pots and pans. Daddy's too mean to buy new ones. Anyway, he was looking especially shifty, going through dustbins and trying to pick the lock on the golden coach, things like that. So I turned to get my telescope so that I could spy on him, and my crown sort of caught on this sticky-out nail and fell out of the window. I think I banged my head, because All Went Black. But I'm sure it fell on to his cart. I didn't tell Daddy because he would have sent out the guards and they would have caught him right away and I wouldn't be having this adventure.'

'You're right!' shouted Iggy, choking in his excitement. 'I have some very valuable information. It *did* fall on his cart. It's hidden in a sack of old rags. I saw it glittering. Besides, he kept boasting he had treasure, though he wouldn't say what it was.'

'I knew I was right,' nodded Matilda. 'You can't be a good detective without hunches.'

Hunches?

What hunches?

Matilda's dress was a bit bunched up at the back, but she didn't look as though she had a hunch. Perhaps she meant lunches.

'I agree,' said Iggy, munching away happily. 'I always enjoy my food. Some don't bother with lunch, but Dragons . . .' He was talking to an empty space. Matilda had gone.

He caught up with her a few seconds later. She was triumphantly waving Shamus O'Shifty's dirty red hanky.

'A clue!' she said. 'He can't be far ahead, it's still fresh. Justice will soon be done.'

'How? What's the plan? Can I help?' said Iggy.

Matilda looked thoughtful. 'I haven't quite decided on the plan,' she admitted. 'But yes, you might come in very useful. Let's go, pardner.'

And off they went. Iggy was sad to cut short his lunch, but thrilled that Matilda thought he might come in useful.

As the morning wore on and still the trail continued, they began to tire. Matilda's moustache developed a distinct droop, and finally dropped off altogether.

'Bother!' she said. 'The glue's melted. I'll have to try something else.'

She turned her back and busied herself with her bag for a moment or two. When she turned round, she was wearing a large pair of black framed plastic glasses with a false nose attached.

'There. Recognise me?'

'Well – yes,' admitted Iggy. 'But only because of your voice,' he fibbed loyally.

'That's all right then. I can disguise that when I have to.'

They were reaching the edge of the forest, and the trees were beginning to thin out. A cluster of cottages appeared a short way ahead.

'Foiled!' sighed Matilda. 'I wanted to catch up with him before he reached the village.'

'Why?'

'He may have friends there. He might give the crown to a fence.'

Iggy stared around, hoping to see the crown dangling from a fence somewhere.

'Not *that* sort of fence, silly. A fence is someone who receives stolen goods. Don't just stand there, Iggy, we'll have to hurry. What are you staring at?'

'Matilda,' said Iggy. 'Your nose has gone.'

'Oh blow that nose! It must have come loose again, I'm always fixing it. Wait there, lie low, and look for clues. I'll nip back and find it. It can't be far away.' And off she went.

Iggy stretched out beneath the trees and stared, fascinated, at the People village. It was a pretty village. Each thatched cottage had a tidy garden full of golden daffodils. The villagers were obviously very proud of their daffodils. They grew in every window box, and double rows of them were planted along the verge of the cobbled street. Behind the village, on the top of a hill, jutted the ruined castle Iggy had spotted from the peak of his mountain. All was very quiet and peaceful. Perhaps the People were asleep in their cottages.

Suddenly, the peace was shattered.

'That's him, boys! That's the fire hazard! Quick, before he escapes!'

It was Shamus O'Shifty!

Iggy started up – but too late. A huge net descended on him from the trees above his head, hopelessly tangling his wings and feet. People rushed at him from everywhere, waving pitchforks, sticks, buckets, and lengths of rope.

'The water, lads!' screamed O'Shifty's voice. 'Quick! Put his fires out!'

And a deluge of freezing water poured down his throat as he opened his mouth to bite through the net. It met up with the fires in his belly, causing a large amount of hissing and steaming as well as a chronic attack of hiccups. Dragons really shouldn't drink water, remember?

'Bonk him! Bonk him over the head!' howled the hateful O'Shifty.

And somebody must have done just that, because Iggy felt a painful blow on the back of his neck. He saw stars, moons, and even a pigeon or two before he discovered the meaning of *All Went Black*.

## 4

## A Knight in Jail

Iggy was woken by a combination of things. Some-thing small that squeaked was biting his tail. Something wet and cold was dribbling down his back. Something clanked and jingled as he tried to move into a sitting position. Worst of all, though, somebody was singing in a grim, ghastly drone.

*Sing ho! For the Life of a Jailor,*
*A Life far removed from the sun,*
*The clink of the chains and the stink of the drains,*
*Now that's what a jailor calls fun.*

*Sing ho! For the rats and the spiders,*
*The sound of the jangling keys,*
*For what can be better than padlocks and fetters*
*And one or two prisoners to tease?*

*Sing ho . . .*

Luckily we are spared the rest – for Iggy hiccuped and the song stopped.

'Well, well, well,' growled the singer. 'Awake are we? All blinky winky and ready to greet a new day. Good morning, mummy, is my breakfast ready? Is the sun shining? Her, her, her, her.'

The hoarse voice broke into a rusty giggle. Iggy

rubbed his eyes, shushed away the rat nibbling his tail, and tried to move away from the water pouring down the wall at his back. He couldn't. He was attached by a dozen stout chains and padlocks to the stone walls of a small, windowless cell. The floor was a good inch deep in smelly, stagnant water. One of the walls was barred and a padlocked door was set in the middle. Through the bars peered a face.

'Meet your friendly jailor,' it said. ''Orrible ain't I?'

He was.

Thick eyebrows met in the middle over a pair of mean, bloodshot eyes. The right eye worked normally. The left permanantly gazed inwards towards the nose which resembled a potato. Beneath the nose the grinning, blubbery mouth revealed two chipped black teeth. Enormous ears stuck out like watering-can handles on either side – and to crown it all, the head was completely bald.

'You'll 'ave to get used to it,' continued the jailor. 'It's all you'll be seeing from now on. Joe Jangles is the name. I'm the boss round 'ere, and what I says goes. Got that, flower?'

'Got it,' said Iggy. 'Er – where am I?'

'The castle dungeon, flower. Where else? 'Ere's where they stick all the trouble makers. Uncle Joe looks after 'em. 'Ome from 'ome it is. I suppose we're a bit peckish?'

'Starving!' confessed Iggy. The water that had gone down his throat had completely put his fires out, and he was ravenous.

'No doubt. Now, tell yer Uncle Joe. What is it you lizards like to eat?'

'Firewood,' Iggy told him. 'And coal, of course, if there's any going spare. By the way, I'm a Dragon, not a lizard. My name's Big Iggy.'

'It's all the same to me, flower. I'm a bit short sighted. Well now. Let's see what we can find, eh?'

The jailor moved away from the bars. At every step, there was a jingling and jangling from the huge bunch of assorted keys, padlocks and hand-cuffs that hung from his belt.

Iggy craned forward in order to see what lay beyond his cell. Flaming torches flickered, casting enormous shadows as Joe Jangles moved around, humming and giggling to himself. A flight of curving stone steps led upwards to freedom and the open air. A stout oak table was set to one side of the steps, displaying a dented truncheon, a jam dough-nut and a very unflattering framed portrait of a mad rhino – or, was it Mrs Jangles? To the left of the steps was a cupboard, at which Joe Jangles was busying himself. His rear view was horrible too. Folds of flesh creased his thick red neck. A leather jerkin strained across his massive back. Coarse trousers covered his bulging backside, and his dumpy legs ended in the sort of boots that bullies wear and ballet dancers don't.

When he finally turned round, he was holding a tray containing a mug of water, a piece of green, stale bread, and a small grey chunk of hard cheese.

'Now, ain't that yummy?' gasped Joe Jangles, nearly dying with laughter. 'A feast for the fangs, that. Now, you behave yerself, flower, and Uncle Joe'll give you yer nice supper.'

But before he could do any such thing, a shout echoed down the stone stairway.

'Another one for yer, Mr Jangles. Parkin' offence this time. All right if us comes down?'

'Password!' bellowed Joe Jangles.

'Daffydils.'

'All right. Come on down.'

That's when another voice piped up. It was reedy, high, and sounded very annoyed. It said things like:

'Unhand me, fellow!' and 'I say, do you jolly well *mind*?' and 'You'll be sowwy about this, mark my words!' and 'Oh no! Not my sword! That's wotten!'

'Well, well, well,' drooled Joe Jangles, plonking the tray back down on the table. 'Another little playmate fer Uncle Joe, eh? It never rains but it pours.'

There was a sudden high pitched shriek, followed by a sound rather like dozens of sauce-pans rolling down a cobblestone hill. Iggy watched in fascination as a figure in a full suit of armour came hurtling round the bend, landing with a crash at Joe Jangles' feet. Behind the figure came two burly, frowning villagers, both holding pitchforks. One of them held a sword.

'Yer welcome to this un, Joe,' said the sword holder. "E be a right charly. Deserves to be put away. Parks 'is 'orse on a double yeller line o' daffydils. Flippin' beast wuz tuckin' in good an' proper. Cheek.'

'Then 'e starts complainin' an' throwin' 'is weight about when Seth 'ere politely smashes 'im over the 'ead,' added the second. 'Thinks 'e's better 'n the rest of us. Snob.'

'I say, that's jolly unfair!'

The snob in armour struggled noisily to his feet and removed his helmet, revealing himself as a haughty looking young man with flowing fair hair and bulging grey eyes. His nostrils flared, his mouth pouted, and his chin receded shyly behind one of those whispy, hopeful little beards.

'Jolly unfair, I say!' he repeated crossly.

'Tain't,' argued the one called Seth. 'You think we be country bumpkins, don't yer, toffee nose? Think we be peasants.'

'No I don't, you beastly peasant. Give me back my sword. Sir Weginald goes nowhere without his sword.'

'Well, 'e's goin' in that there cell wivout it,' broke in Joe Jangles, taking the sword from the villager. 'This stays wiv me. This'll join Uncle Joe's collection. All right, gents. Leave 'im ter me.'

'Good riddance,' muttered the villagers, departing. 'Swankpot.'

'Bumpkins! Peasants! Wuffians!' shrieked Sir Reginald. Then:

'Here! What in the blazes are you playing at, you fat oaf!'

''Andcuffin' yer, flower,' said Joe Jangles, doing it. 'An' any more of that fat oaf talk and Uncle Joe'll stick yer in wiv the Dragon.'

'Dwagon? What Dwagon?' Sir Reginald whirled around and laid eyes on Iggy for the first time.

'Hello,' said Iggy pleasantly.

'By jove! Th-that's it! The Dwagon that Kidnapped Her Woyal Highness! Come out, you wotter, and fight!'

'I did nothing of the kind,' protested Iggy indignantly.

'Oh yes you jolly well did! I saw your gweat big claw marks wight next to her footpwints in the fowest. I've been twailing you. What have you done with her, you overgwown worm? Hey – do you *mind*! Get your gweasy fingers awf my clean chainmail . . . get *awf*, I say . . . ouch . . .'

This was followed by a lot of clunking and clattering, the slamming of a door and the final-sounding turning of a key in a lock.

'Now, you quit yer hollerin', Reggie boy,' growled Joe Jangles. 'Uncle Joe's off ter put this 'ere sword wiv his collection, see. When I get back, I'm 'avin' me supper. Then, if I'm in a good mood, I might give you *your* supper. I'll leave you boys ter get acquainted. Her, her, her, her.'

And his plonking footsteps shambled off into the distance.

'Consider yourself vewy lucky that wotter didn't put me in with you!' shouted Sir Reginald from the cell next door. 'I'd have pulvewized you by now. Kidnapper!'

'Oh, do stop all this rubbish,' sighed Iggy. 'Matilda's a friend. Why would I kidnap her?'

'Wansom money,' snapped Sir Reginald. 'Or lunch.'

'Don't be silly. Dragons don't eat Princesses. Not any more.'

'Liar.'

Iggy was so fed up, he didn't even bother to reply.

'What have you done with her?' persisted Sir Reginald, rattling the bars and getting himself terribly worked up. 'Just you wait till her father gets to hear about it. He's King, you know.'

'I know,' said Iggy. 'She told me.'

'Yes, well he's not going to take kindly to this. His daughter kidnapped and his best knight impwisoned. He'll be pwetty cwoss, I can tell you.'

'Look,' said Iggy wearily. 'Matilda's crown got stolen by Shamus O'Shifty. She was trailing him. We met in the forest. She said I might come in useful. Then I got captured because O'Shifty said I was a fire hazard, but really he wanted me out of the way because he knew I knew he had the crown. That's the truth.'

'So where is she now?'

'I don't know. Looking for her nose.'

'Her *what*?'

'Her false nose.'

'Oh. Wight. One of her silly disguises, I suppose.' Sir Reginald sounded a bit calmer. 'I suppose it could be twue. She's always sneaking awf on adventures. The King gets fuwious. It's always me who has to go wushing awf after her. I get pwetty sick of it sometimes. I never seem to get a decent quest.'

'Tch, tch, tch,' sympathised Iggy.

Encouraged, Sir Reginald went on. 'She does it on purpose, you know. Leaves things lying awound to tempt wobbers. She likes being wobbed.'

'Not the crown,' said Iggy. 'It fell out of the window by accident. Into O'Shifty's cart.'

'Oh yah? Hah! She pwobably thwew it down. Just to give herself an excuse to sneak awf and spoil my day. I'd planned to do all sorts of things. Lie in. Late bweakfast. Spot of gentle jousting. Not wot in a stinking dungeon.'

'Sorry – *what* in a stinking dungeon?'

'Wot! Wot, cloth ears! Look, when are you going to do something about getting us out of here? I don't know about your cell, but mine's knee deep in water. Listen.' There was a sloshing noise. 'See?'

'There's nothing I'd like better,' sighed Iggy. 'If I knew how.'

'Good gwacious! You're a Dwagon, aren't you? Burn thwough the bars or something.'

'I can't,' confessed Iggy. 'They put my fires out. I need to eat at least half a ton of firewood before I can produce a single spark. Sorry.'

'Useless,' muttered Sir Reginald. 'If only I had my sword . . .'

'Well yer don't, flower,' broke in Joe Jangles. 'Cos it's mine now.'

He was standing by his table holding a steaming bowl of thick, grey, splodgy stuff with what looked like bits of old bath sponge floating on top.

'The wife's stew,' he explained. 'Delicious, eh? I expect you're jealous.' And he slumped into his chair and scooped great handfuls into his mouth, making disgusting slurpy, globby noises while Iggy and Sir Reginald tried not to watch. Two minutes later the bowl was empty. He gave a huge belch, and stretched.

'I say, fellow! What about ours?' enquired Sir Reginald sharply.

'You? Oh, yes, of course. You're waiting for yours, aren't you? Well, it's all ready.'

Joe Jangles stood up, belched again, and picked up the tray containing the bread, cheese and water. He gave a broad grin, tittered . . . and dropped it! The water splashed all over the floor, the bread rolled into a puddle, and the cheese shattered into a thousand pieces.

'Oops,' chortled Joe Jangles. 'Butterfingers me.'

'I pwotest!' raged Sir Reginald, clattering and sloshing bitterly. 'I demand my wights!'

Whether he would have got them or not, we will never know – for, just then, more footsteps were heard descending the stone steps.

'Rats' tails! There's no peace down here today!' grumbled Joe Jangles. 'Who's that now? Identify yerself!'

'Jail Inspector,' barked a bossy voice.

'Eh?' said Joe Jangles. 'Who?'

'You heard. Jail Inspector. Come along, man, look lively!'

'Ain't heard nothing about no Jail Inspector,' growled Joe Jangles suspiciously. 'If you're who you say you are, what's the password?'

'Daffodils, of course.'

'Oh. Right,' said Joe Jangles, looking scared and cringing a lot. 'Oh, come on down, sir, do. You'll have to take me as you find me, as the saying goes, ha, ha, ha . . .'

He bowed so low, his head was hanging down around his knees, so he missed the entrance of the Jail Inspector. Iggy and Sir Reginald didn't, however. Their eyes bulged as they took in the long black cloak, the tall hat, the short red hair, black bushy beard, AND THE GRUBBY VELVET DRAWSTRING BAG!

'Oh no!' whispered Iggy. 'She'll never get away with it!'

'Take you as I find you eh? Well, I find you very

smelly,' snapped Matilda. 'What are you doing with your nose in that puddle? Stand up man. These dungeons are a disgrace. I've seen some dungeons in my time, but these are the filthiest yet. Don't you ever clean up?'

Joe Jangles mumbled something about a bad back and shifted from boot to boot, hanging his head.

'That's no excuse. Let me see your keys. Rusty, I suppose.'

Joe Jangles hastily fussed around with his belt and unclipped the bunch of keys, dropping them in a puddle in his hurry to pass them over.

'Leave them!' ordered Matilda. 'Do you think I'm going to examine them like that? They're all covered in stew or something. Go and get something to wipe them with.'

Joe Jangles hesitated. He'd never been parted from his keys. He even slept with them. His wife complained terribly. He wouldn't even let the baby play with them as a rattle. And now this jumped-up, red-haired, bearded midget was demanding that he leave them. That he actually let them out of his sight. He was undecided what to do.

'And while you're about it,' added Matilda briskly. 'Get a mop and bucket. You're going to get this place as clean as a new pin before I leave, or I shall report you to the R.S.P.S.D.'

'Who?' said Joe Jangles, bewildered.

'The Royal Society for the Prevention of Slobs in Dungeons. Hurry up!'

Joe Jangles hurried. Imagine being reported to a society with a name like that. What would they do if they found him guilty? Suppose ... aaaaah! Suppose he was *imprisoned in a dungeon as punishment? Suppose that dungeon was as dirty as this one, and the jailor as mean as he was?* He hurried all right.

As soon as he had disappeared, Iggy, Matilda and Sir Reginald breathed again. It had been touch and go.

'Well done, Matilda,' hissed Iggy. 'Quick – the keys.'

'I say! Tewific. Well done, Your Woyal Highness, that weally was tewwibly good ...'

'Oh, do stop wittering on, Reggie,' said Matilda with a glare. 'I might have known you'd be here. Don't you ever get bored with hanging around snooping on me? Apart from anything else, I get sick and tired of having to rescue you. It's supposed to be the other way round. Uggh. These keys are disgusting. I wonder which one opens Iggy's cell ...'

'Do me first,' suggested Sir Reginald in a very unknightly way. 'I wecognise mine ...'

'Certainly not. Wait your turn. You haven't done anything to help on this adventure. All you've done is get in the way.'

'What about him then?' sulked Sir Reginald. 'What's he done to help?'

'Lots. He spotted the crown for a start. I see you've had your sword taken away again. How many times is that now?'

Sir Reginald didn't reply.

'How did you know the password, Matilda?' asked Iggy excitedly as Matilda finally got his door open and attended to the padlocked chains.

'Oh, you know. Spying and stalking, that sort of thing. I enjoyed the dressing-up best. I got the hat and cloak off O'Shifty's cart while he was in the inn celebrating your capture. Oh, and the crown, of course. It's in my bag. You should have heard the lies he told, Iggy, about how you attacked him and stole his sausages, then tried to set fire to his cart.'

'And to think I thought he was being friendly,' mourned Iggy.

Then ... ''Ere! What's going on?'

It was Joe Jangles. He was standing, open-mouthed, holding a mop and bucket. He was wearing a flowery apron, which belonged to Mrs Jangles, over his leather jacket. A can of something called Dungeon Freshener was tucked under his arm.

You had to hand it to Matilda. She didn't panic.

'I'm inspecting these chains,' she snapped. 'They're disgraceful. Don't just stand there, man.

Get started on that filthy floor.' Her fingers were trembling as she fumbled with the padlocks. She might have got away with it if it wasn't for Sir Reginald, whose nerve finally snapped.

'Me!' he screeched, clanking and sloshing. 'Me, Matilda! Me, ME!'

'I'll do no such thing,' retorted Joe Jangles, advancing. 'You think I'm stupid? I don't believe you're no Jail Inspector. What's going on?'

'You're absolutely right,' said Matilda, breathing again as the last chain fell away. 'No, I'm not a Jail Inspector. Yes, I think you're stupid. And what's going on is a breakout. *Do* shut up, Reggie. Right, Iggy – you're free. Get him!'

Iggy would have liked to have sprung from his cell. It would have fitted the occasion better. The door was so small, he had to squeeze, which wasn't so dramatic, but it was enough to frighten Joe Jangles, who backed away, his face pale under the dirt. It's no joke being confronted by a squeezing green Dragon, even if its fires are out. Something to do with The Size. It doesn't help if you're wearing a flowery apron either. He held up the mop more in self defence than anything, and gave a weak titter when Iggy stretched out a claw, gently took it away, and snapped it in two like a matchstick before popping it in his mouth.

'Now,' said Iggy, pleasantly but firmly. 'Are you going to be reasonable and sit quietly while we chain you up? Or do I have to sit on you?'

Joe Jangles was a broken man. Humbly he shuffled into Iggy's cell, and held out his hands.

'I'll take the first,' he whispered meekly. 'Sir.'

Meanwhile, what had become of Shamus O'Shifty? Right now, he was tiptoeing down the stairway of the inn, feeling very pleased with himself. He had cleverly got that nosey Dragon clapped in jail. He had spent an evening in the inn telling his story to the admiring locals, and had enjoyed a huge, greedy supper and a comfortable night in a proper feather bed. Now, by sneaking out early, he was avoiding paying. When he got to the first big town later that day, he would sell the crown and live the life of a lord. No more pots and pans for Shamus O'Shifty, tee hee.

The previous night, he had debated whether the crown would be safer in his room or on the cart. Finally, he had decided to leave it where it was. Nobody would ever suspect that there was something valuable hidden amongst all the old junk he carted round. But, just to be doubly sure, he had paid that funny little red haired chap with the beard a few pence to keep an eye on it overnight. It never hurt to be too careful.

He reached the front door, opened it silently, and stepped outside. Nobody was about. A solitary horse was wandering down the street, its mouth crammed full of daffodils, but Shamus O'Shifty only gave it a passing glance. He made straight for his cart, which was parked where he had left it, outside the inn. Funnily enough, there was no sign of the strange little man. Shamus O'Shifty felt a sudden chill go through him – and it wasn't the morning air.

Muttering to himself, he scrabbled through the sacks until he found the one he wanted. He felt it. He rummaged through it. He emptied it on the ground, and turned it inside out. All to no avail. The crown had gone.

To add to his troubles, an upstairs window shot open, and the landlady looked out.

'Hey! What about my money, you!'

With a hiss of fury, Shamus O'Shifty took to his heels.

At the same moment, Iggy and Matilda and Sir Reginald were standing outside the walls of the tumbledown castle, enjoying the smell of freedom and planning what to do next.

'Go home and dwy off,' said Sir Reginald. 'My armour's going wusty.'

'Eat,' said Iggy, swallowing the last of the flaming torches which he had snatched from the walls before racing up the steps. 'Find a forest of firewood and eat it.'

'Teach Shamus O'Shifty a lesson,' announced Matilda firmly. 'He'll have discovered the crown's gone missing by now. We'll have to trail him. Goody, this adventure won't end for *weeks*.'

'Oh yes it will,' said Sir Reginald.

'How do you know, tin legs?' sneered Matilda rudely. 'Listen to him, Iggy. He can't wait to drag me off home so Daddy can give him another medal. He always wants to ruin my fun ...'

'I know,' announced Sir Reginald smugly, 'because there's O'Shifty, pushing his handcart over that hill, about five minutes away.'

Sure enough, he was right.

'STOP THIEF!' howled Matilda, setting off in pursuit. Wig, hat and bushy beard scattered to the four winds. Considering the cloak was four sizes too big, she did quite well to get as far as she did (about six paces) before falling flat on her face. Sir Reginald came gamely clattering up behind (it's not easy to sprint in a suit of armour) and, naturally, tripped over her. Neither was hurt, but both were winded and unable to speak. That left Iggy – and, as we know, Dragons find it uncomfortable to walk, let alone run. They can fly, though. If they keep their eyes wide open.

Iggy did a waddling little run, stretched wide his wings, jumped . . .

### AND SOARED!

Shamus O'Shifty had heard Matilda's shout, and seen the three small figures start off in pursuit. He was scuttling along as fast as he could, sparks rising from the handcart wheels, and pots and pans jiggling on their hooks. He kept looking over his shoulder, but it would have been better if he'd looked upwards into the sky. If he had, being dive-bombed by Iggy wouldn't have come as such a shock.

A huge green wing came out of nowhere, and swiped his hat off. It was his third best hat. He'd lost two, remember? That was followed by two strong claws digging into his shoulders. He howled as his feet left the ground and he found himself being carried through the air. Then, he was falling . . . down, down, ever down, landing with a huge CRUMP in a ditch full of mud, nettles, scratchy brambles and rubbish. He banged his head painfully on a rusty old anvil thrown there by a blacksmith. Half a soggy ham roll, abandoned by some careless picnicker, lodged in his ear, and worst of all, the piece of string which held up his trousers snapped. There he lay, kicking feebly, and watched helplessly as Iggy seized the cart with all four claws and rose with it effortlessly into the air like a great green kite. He did it as easily as you or I would pick up a dropped take-away fried chicken box and place it in a dustbin. Except that he didn't put the cart in a dustbin. Instead, he gently placed it at the top of the tallest tree he could find. Then, dusting his claws off, he glided back to where Matilda and Sir Reginald were sitting up rubbing their bruised (or, in Sir Reginald's case, dented) knees. Slowly, gracefully, Iggy landed.

'Iggy!' gasped Matilda. 'That was simply brilliant.'

'It was nothing,' said Iggy shyly. 'I think I'm getting the hang of this Flying business now.'

'That's it, then, I suppose,' sighed Matilda regretfully. 'Justice is done. End of adventure.'

'I should jolly well hope so,' sniffed Sir Reginald. 'Come on. I'd better get you home. Your father will be hopping mad by now.'

'How will you get there?' asked Iggy.

'On my twusty steed, of course,' replied Sir Reginald sniffily. 'I am a knight, you know. It's a standard piece of equipment.' And he put two fingers to his mouth and blew a shrill whistle. After a moment, there was the sound of hooves, and the

haughtiest looking horse you've ever seen saun-
tered from a nearby clump of trees. It had a daffodil dangling from its mouth, and looked down its
nose at all three of them.

'Come on, Wuss,' coaxed Sir Reginald. 'Over
here, old fellow. Did you miss your master?'

Russ sighed and looked away.

'You will come back with us, won't you, Iggy?'
asked Matilda. 'I'm sure Daddy will want to thank
you. After all, I was the detective, but you're the
hero of this adventure. Reggie will try and pretend
he did it all, but I shall tell Daddy he just got in the
way as usual.'

Sir Reginald didn't hear the last remark. He
was too busy trying to stop Russ walking away
from him every time he tried to mount.

'It's very kind of you, Matilda,' said Iggy. 'But
I think I'd better be getting on. I must find the
Land of the Dragon, you see. If I come back to the
palace with you, I'll keep getting involved in your
adventures instead of my own. But I promise to
keep in touch. I'll send you a postcard.'

'All right,' sighed Matilda. 'But I do hate
saying goodbye. All the standing around not
knowing what to say . . .'

But she didn't get the chance to say any more.
There were angry shouts, and a crowd of furious
villagers came charging over the hill. They were
yelling all sorts of things about escaped convicts

and fire hazards and thieving tinkers and false jail inspectors and daffodil-eating horses and snobby knights who fancied themselves, and so on.

'Oops!' said Iggy.' 'I'm taking off. Bye bye, folks.'

'Goodbye, Iggy. Don't forget the postcard. Oh, do *hurry up*, Reggie, you're absolutely useless. Look, I'll hold its tail, you get up. Get *up*, idiot . . .'

Iggy left them to it. He did his little waddling run, and was airborne before you could sneeze. Higher and higher he flew, until the shouts of the villagers died away and all he could hear was the wind whistling past and the song of the skylarks wheeling about him as he rode the morning breeze.

Far below, he saw a small, bedraggled figure haul itself out of a ditch and shake its fist skywards. He saw the tumbledown castle. He saw the deserted village bereft of every single daffodil. He saw Sir Reginald and Matilda galloping along, waving and laughing up at him as the disdainful Russ put more and more distance between them and the irate villagers. He saw the forest. With a twinge of guilt, he saw the burnt-up glade. He saw the high mountain which was once his home, and the shining palace in the distance, which was Matilda's. Beyond that, the wide river flowed to the horizon. And beyond that? Maybe the Land of the Dragon.

He aimed that way.

# Epilogue

Exactly one year later, two grey squirrels received a huge sack of mixed nuts. It came by Internuta. There was a card attached, and this is what it said:

They guessed who it was from.

On the same day, a carrier pigeon delivered four postcards. The first was to Matilda. The message was written in invisible ink. When she eagerly heated it up, she discovered that it was written in code. Here's what it said:

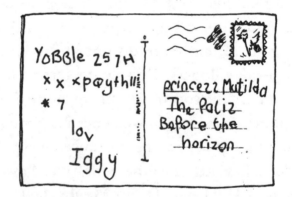

She never did work out what it meant, but spent many happy hours trying.

Here's the second card:

i will get
you won
day

EEgul
top of
Mountain

The card might have puzzled the Eagle if it had been able to read – but, as it was, it came in useful for scraping out the mess made by three baby fledglings who now occupied the nest.

Here's the third card:

flumbo and
2parky dragon
a cave somewhere

We'll never know what the message was, because as you can see, it's been burnt off. That's because Flambo woke after a snooze, yawned and accidentally set fire to the post which had been piling up over the last six months. (Mainly advertisements for Dragon's Digest and final reminder bills from the coalman.) Rather a pity, as the pigeon went to a lot of trouble to track them down.

The last postcard, of course, was for Large Lizzy, and she was very pleased when it arrived. Here it is:

deer Ma,
havink a lovly tim.
Wizh you were heer.
Haffent found Land of
dragon yet, but hav
-ink lots of adventoors.
2 oszigee tazte
nice, did you no? i bite
my scarf, ma. I uzed
it to gag a jaylor i
met. dote worry i
excaped pleze will you
nit me another. Ill coulect,
you are well lots of

Ma (Large
Lizzy dragon)
cave halfway
up mountain.

it in 199 years. hop
love Iggy xxx

'Bless the boy,' said Lizzy, wiping away a tear. And she got out the needles.